ONE THOUSAND DOLLARS
AND OTHER PLAYS

Richard Rockwell's father is one of the richest men in New York. He thinks that money can buy anything you want. It certainly helps with most things, but can it buy love for young Richard?

Bobby Gillian has a different problem. His uncle left him a thousand dollars in his will, and Bobby doesn't know what to spend it on. People think that he is only interested in girls, champagne, and betting on horses, but perhaps there is more to him than that.

For Towers Chandler and Miss Martha, money is less important than love. But they both discover the sad truth that it is only too easy to say or do the wrong thing, and lose their chance of love.

OXFORD BOOKWORMS LIBRARY

Playscripts

One Thousand Dollars
and Other Plays

Stage 2 (700 headwords)

Playscripts Series Editor: Clare West

One Thousand Dollars

and Other Plays

Retold by
John Escott

OXFORD UNIVERSITY PRESS

OXFORD

UNIVERSITY PRESS

Great Clarendon Street, Oxford OX2 6DP

Oxford University Press is a department of the University of Oxford.
It furthers the University's objective of excellence in research, scholarship,
and education by publishing worldwide in

Oxford New York

Auckland Cape Town Dar es Salaam Hong Kong Karachi
Kuala Lumpur Madrid Melbourne Mexico City Nairobi
New Delhi Shanghai Taipei Toronto

With offices in

Argentina Austria Brazil Chile Czech Republic France Greece
Guatemala Hungary Italy Japan Poland Portugal Singapore
South Korea Switzerland Thailand Turkey Ukraine Vietnam

OXFORD and OXFORD ENGLISH are registered trade marks of
Oxford University Press in the UK and in certain other countries

ISBN 978 0 19 423520 4

A complete recording of this Bookworms edition of
One Thousand Dollars and Other Plays is available on audio CD ISBN 978 0 19 423526 6

Printed in Hong Kong

Illustrated by: Susan Scott

For more information on the Oxford Bookworms Library,
visit www.oup.com/bookworms

CONTENTS

INTRODUCTION

A young man is in love with a beautiful girl. But can his rich
father's money help him to marry her?

CHARACTERS IN THE PLAY

Anthony Rockwell, a rich man
Richard Rockwell, his son
Aunt Ellen, Anthony's sister and Richard's aunt
Miss Lantry, a beautiful young woman
Taxi driver
Kelly, a man who works for Anthony Rockwell

PERFORMANCE NOTES

Scene 1: A room at Anthony Rockwell's home, with a desk
and two or three chairs
Scene 2: As Scene 1
Scene 3: As Scene 1
Scene 4: The inside of a taxi, with one long seat at the back,
and a single seat at the front for the driver
Scene 5: In Anthony Rockwell's bedroom, a room with a bed,
a cupboard and two chairs
Scene 6: As Scene 1

You will need a book, a cup, a glass, a ring, and a packet of
sheets of paper (to look like money).

All that Money can Buy

A fine boy

A room at Anthony Rockwell's house in New York. He is sitting at his desk reading. His son, Richard, comes in.

RICHARD   You wanted to see me, father?

ANTHONY   Richard, what do you pay for your suits?

RICHARD   *(Surprised)* About sixty dollars, I think, Dad.

ANTHONY   You're a fine boy. Some young men pay more than a hundred dollars. You have more money than most of them, but you're careful.

RICHARD   *(Sadly)* Yes, Dad.

ANTHONY   Yes, you're a fine boy, and you can thank money for that. Money will do it every time.

Richard sits down in a chair. He looks sad.

RICHARD   There are some things that money can't do.

ANTHONY   Now don't say that. You can buy anything.

RICHARD   Your money can't buy me a way into older and better families than ours.

ANTHONY   *(Angrily)* Can't it? *(Looking closely at Richard)* There's something wrong. What is it?

RICHARD   Well, Dad . . .

ANTHONY   Tell me. I can get ten million dollars in twenty-four hours. I can have a boat ready to take you to the Bahamas in two days. Why aren't you happy?

RICHARD Well . . . there's a girl . . .

ANTHONY (*Interested*) What's her name? You've got money, and you're a nice young man. Take her for a walk, or a ride. Walk home with her from church.

'Why aren't you happy?'

RICHARD You don't know her family. Every hour of her
time is planned days before. I love her, but how
can I tell her? I can't write down all the things
that I want to say.

ANTHONY Are you telling me that you can't get an hour
or two of the girl's time? And with all the money
I've got!

RICHARD It's too late now. In two days she's going to
Europe for two years. I'm going to see her alone
tomorrow evening for seven or eight minutes.

ANTHONY Seven or eight minutes!

RICHARD She's staying in the country at her aunt's.

ANTHONY Go and see her there!

RICHARD I can't. But I'm meeting her at the station with a
taxi tomorrow evening at 8.30. We'll drive to
Wallack's Theatre. She's meeting her mother and
some of her friends there.

ANTHONY *(Looking thoughtful)* It won't take long to
drive down Broadway to the theatre.

RICHARD I know. Will I get time to tell her everything
that I want to tell her? No. No, father, your
money can't help me. It can't buy me one minute
of time.

ANTHONY All right, Richard, my boy. Go out with your
friends now. You say that money can't buy time?
Well, money can buy most things.

True love is everything!

The same room, that evening. Anthony Rockwell is talking to his sister, Ellen. They are sitting in chairs. Ellen has a cup of coffee. Anthony has a glass of something stronger.

ANTHONY He says that ten million dollars can't buy a way into older and better families than ours, Ellen.

ELLEN Anthony, you're always thinking about money. But money is nothing. True love is everything! Why didn't Richard speak to the girl earlier?

ANTHONY I don't know.

ELLEN How could a girl say no to a fine boy like him? And now there's no time. When does she go to Europe?

ANTHONY The day after tomorrow.

'True love is everything!'

ELLEN   Poor Richard! All your money cannot make him happy. Oh dear! Oh dear!

SCENE 3

The ring

The same room, the next evening. Richard is dressed to go out. Ellen is with him. She is giving him a ring.

ELLEN   Wear this ring tonight. Your mother gave it to me. She said that it brought good luck in love. 'Give it to Richard when he falls in love with a girl,' she told me.

Richard tries to put it on his smallest finger, but the ring is too small. He puts it in his coat pocket.

RICHARD   It's too small to wear, but I'll keep it safe.

ELLEN   Good luck, Richard.

RICHARD   Thank you, aunt.

SCENE 4

A lot of traffic

Richard and Miss Lantry are in the back of a taxi. The taxi driver is sitting in front.

MISS LANTRY   We must hurry. Mother doesn't like waiting.

RICHARD *(To the taxi driver)* To Wallack's Theatre. As
quickly as you can, driver!

TAXI DRIVER Yes, sir. *(He starts driving.)*

RICHARD I want to tell you—

MISS LANTRY *(Looking out of the taxi)* Where are we?

RICHARD What? Oh, we're turning from Forty-Second
Street into Broadway. But I wanted to tell you—

MISS LANTRY How long will it take to get to the theatre?

RICHARD Seven or eight minutes. *(He takes the ring from
his pocket.)* I want to show you – oh! *(He drops
the ring and it falls out of the taxi window.)*
Driver, stop! Stop!

MISS LANTRY What is it?

RICHARD I've dropped a ring. It was my mother's. I must
look for it. I don't want to lose it. It won't take a
minute.

*Richard gets out of the taxi and looks on the ground.
Miss Lantry looks worriedly at her watch. The taxi
driver is looking round him in surprise. Traffic noises are
heard. After a minute, Richard comes back.*

RICHARD I've got it! On you go, driver.

TAXI DRIVER Sorry, sir. But I can't.

MISS LANTRY Why don't you drive on? We'll be late.

RICHARD *(Standing up in the taxi and looking round)* Has
all the traffic in New York stopped around us?
Where did it all come from?

6

'I've got it!'

TAXI DRIVER I don't know, sir.

MISS LANTRY Where are the police? Can't they help?

RICHARD I'm very sorry. We can't go on, and it'll take an
hour to move all this traffic away!

MISS LANTRY Show me the ring. We can't help this.
(*Smiling*) And I don't like theatres very much.

7

True love

Anthony Rockwell's bedroom. He is sitting up in bed reading. There is a knock at the door.

ANTHONY   Who is it?

ELLEN   It's me.

ANTHONY   Come in, Ellen.

Ellen comes into the room. She looks excited.

ELLEN   She is going to marry our Richard!

Anthony smiles. He does not look surprised.

ANTHONY   Oh? Is that right?

Ellen sits down on a chair near the bed.

ELLEN   They had to stop on the way to the theatre. And what stopped them? Not your money! It was a little ring!

ANTHONY   (*Still smiling*) What happened? Tell me.

ELLEN   Richard dropped the ring in the street. He got out to find it, and suddenly there was traffic everywhere!

ANTHONY   How strange!

ELLEN   Yes! It was two hours before the taxi could move again! So he had time to tell her that he loved her.

ANTHONY   And they're going to marry, are they? Well, I'm happy to hear it.

ELLEN   Don't ever say 'Money can buy anything!' to me
again, Anthony. Not after tonight. It isn't true.
Money is nothing when you have true love.

SCENE 6
A good day's work

Next morning. Anthony is in his study. With him is Kelly.

ANTHONY   Thank you, Kelly. That was a good day's work.
Now, what did I give you? Five thousand dollars?

KELLY   Yes, Mr Rockwell, and I paid out three hundred
dollars of my own money. I got the taxis for five
dollars, but the other drivers wanted ten dollars.
But the police were the worst.

ANTHONY   Were they?

KELLY   Yes. They wanted fifty dollars. But everything
went beautifully, Mr Rockwell. Everybody arrived
at the right time. It was two hours before anybody
moved!

Rockwell gives Kelly a packet, with money inside it.

ANTHONY   Here you are, Kelly. One thousand for your
work, and your three hundred back. OK?

KELLY   Thank you.

ANTHONY   (*Laughing*) Thank *you*, Kelly. Money talks,
right?

INTRODUCTION

A young man's uncle leaves him one thousand dollars in his will. What can the young man do with it?

CHARACTERS IN THE PLAY

Bobby Gillian, a young man
Mr Tolman, a lawyer
Mr Sharp, a lawyer
Miss Hayden, a pretty young woman
Miss Lotta Lauriere, a dancer
Bryson, a man of forty
Man at the theatre

PERFORMANCE NOTES

Scene 1:   A lawyers' office, with a desk and two chairs
Scene 2:   A restaurant, with tables and chairs
Scene 3:   Theatre dressing room, with a dressing table, clothes cupboard and a mirror
Scene 4:   As Scene 1
Scene 5:   The living room in Bobby's uncle's house, with a table and chair
Scene 6:   As Scene 1

You will need a piece of paper that looks like a will, another piece of paper with writing on it, some writing paper, a pen, a packet of money, a book, and a cup.

One Thousand Dollars

The will

*In Tolman and Sharp's office. Mr Tolman is sitting
behind his desk. He has just finished reading a will.
Bobby Gillian is sitting the other side of the desk.*

TOLMAN Well, there you are. Your uncle wrote his will a
month or two before he died, and now I've read it
to you. What do you think?

11

BOBBY (*Laughing*) It's not going to be easy to spend a
thousand dollars. Fifty dollars or fifty thousand
would be easier. I'll have to ask a friend how to
spend it.

TOLMAN Did you listen carefully when I was reading the
will? After spending the thousand dollars, you
must tell me, in writing, how you spent it. Will
you do that?

BOBBY Yes, I'll do it, Mr Tolman.

TOLMAN (*Giving Bobby a packet*) Then here's the money.
One thousand dollars.

SCENE 2
A lot or very little

*At a restaurant. Bryson is sitting at a table, drinking coffee
and reading a book. Bobby sits down opposite him.*

BOBBY Hello there, Bryson! Put down your book, I've
got a funny story to tell you!

BRYSON Tell it to somebody at one of the other tables.
You know I don't like your stories.

BOBBY It's a good story. I've just come from my uncle
Septimus's lawyers. He's died and left me one
thousand dollars! What can I do with it?

BRYSON I thought old man Gillian had half a million.

'I've got a funny story to tell you!'

BOBBY   He did. He left most of it to the hospital that killed him! Isn't that funny? His secretary gets ten dollars, and I get a thousand.

BRYSON   You've always got plenty of money to spend.

BOBBY   Lots. Uncle Septimus was like Father Christmas to me.

BRYSON   Did he have any other family?

BOBBY   None. There is a Miss Hayden who lives in his house. She's a quiet little thing. The daughter of one of my uncle's friends. I forgot to say that she got ten dollars, too.

BRYSON   Did she?

BOBBY   Why didn't he leave me just ten dollars? Then I could spend it on two bottles of champagne and forget Uncle Septimus and his money.

BRYSON (*Smiling*) A thousand dollars can be a lot or very little. One man could buy a happy home with it and laugh at America's richest man.

BOBBY   That's true.

BRYSON A thousand dollars could buy milk for one hundred babies this summer, and save fifty of their lives. It could send a clever boy to college.

BOBBY   Listen, Bryson. I asked you to tell me what *I* could do with a thousand dollars.

BRYSON (*Laughing*) Go and buy a gold necklace for your favourite dancer, Lotta Lauriere. Then go and work on a farm. Work with sheep. I've never liked sheep.

BOBBY   The beautiful Lotta! Yes, you're right. I want to spend all the money on one thing. You see, I've got to write and say what I spent it on, and I don't like writing. Thanks, Bryson!

SCENE 3
A necklace for Lotta

Lotta Lauriere's dressing room at the theatre. She is getting ready. There is a knock at the door.

14

'Who is it?'

LOTTA Who is it?

BOBBY It's me. Bobby Gillian.

LOTTA Come in, Bobby. (*He comes in.*) What is it, Bobby? I have to go and dance in two minutes.

BOBBY Listen, Lotta. Would you like a pretty necklace? I can spend a thousand. What do you say to that?

LOTTA (*Laughing*) Oh, you sweet man! It's true that I love pretty things. But . . .

BOBBY Yes?

LOTTA (*Putting on a hat*) Did you see the necklace that Della Stacey was wearing the other night? It cost more than two thousand dollars at Tiffany's.

BOBBY Oh, did it?

There is a knock on the door. A man comes in.

MAN Miss Lauriere, it's time!

LOTTA Oh! I must go, Bobby!

Lotta leaves. The man waits for Bobby to leave.

BOBBY What would *you* do with a thousand dollars?

MAN Open a bar. I know a place that could make a lot of money. Are you thinking of putting some money into— ?

BOBBY Oh, no. I only wanted to know.

MAN Listen, this could make us both a lot of money.

BOBBY Excuse me. I must go.

Bobby leaves the room.

MAN And I thought it was my lucky day.

Bobby asks a question

*In Tolman and Sharp's office. Tolman is sitting at his
desk. Bobby is standing the other side of Tolman's desk.
The lawyer does not look pleased to see him.*

TOLMAN What do you want now, Mr Gillian?
BOBBY Can I ask you a question? Did my uncle leave
        Miss Hayden more than the ten dollars?
TOLMAN No, he didn't.
BOBBY Thank you very much, sir.
TOLMAN Is that all?
BOBBY Yes, thank you. That's all I wanted to know.

SCENE 5
News for Miss Hayden

*In Septimus Gillian's living room. Miss Hayden is sitting
at a table, writing letters. She looks up when Bobby
comes in.*

BOBBY I've just come from old Tolman's. They found a –
        what's the word? – a codicil to the will.
MISS HAYDEN They did?
BOBBY Dear old uncle left you some more money. A

thousand dollars. Tolman asked me to bring it to you. Here it is. (*He puts the packet of money on the table.*)

MISS HAYDEN   Oh! Oh!

BOBBY   I love you, Miss Hayden. Did you know that?

MISS HAYDEN   Oh! No. I am sorry.

BOBBY   Is there no hope for me?

MISS HAYDEN   I – no, I am sorry.

BOBBY   (*Smiling*) Can I write a note?

MISS HAYDEN   Of course. (*She gives him a pen and some paper.*) I – please, excuse me.

She leaves. Bobby writes a short note, then reads it.

BOBBY   (*Reading*) 'Paid to the best and dearest woman in the world, one thousand dollars. For all the happiness she brings to people.'

SCENE 6
Another fifty thousand!

In Tolman and Sharp's office. Tolman is sitting behind his desk when Bobby comes into the room.

BOBBY   I've spent the thousand dollars. And I've got a note to tell you what I spent it on.

He puts the note on Tolman's desk. Tolman gets up and goes to the door. He opens it.

'Is there no hope for me?'

TOLMAN   (*Calling*) Sharp! Come in here, please.

SHARP   (*Coming into the room*) Yes? (*He looks at Bobby, then looks down at the note.*) Oh. I understand.

He goes out of the room again. Tolman and Bobby wait silently. Sharp comes back with a piece of paper. The two lawyers read it and look at each other.

TOLMAN   Mr Gillian, there was a codicil to your uncle's will.

BOBBY   A codicil?

TOLMAN   We were told not to read it until you told us, in writing, how you spent the thousand dollars. You have now done this, so I will tell you what the codicil says.

BOBBY   Please do.

TOLMAN   Your uncle tells us in the codicil that we can give you another fifty thousand dollars—

BOBBY   (*Very surprised*) What!

TOLMAN   (*Continuing*) —if you have used the money to do some good for others. But . . .

BOBBY   But?

TOLMAN   If you have spent it carelessly or given it away to the wrong people—

BOBBY   (*Laughing*) As I usually do!

TOLMAN   Then the fifty thousand dollars must be paid to Miss Miriam Hayden. Now, Mr Gillian. Mr Sharp and I will read your note and find out—

Bobby quickly takes the note from the desk.

BOBBY (*Smiling*) It's all right. There's no need to read it.
I lost the thousand dollars betting on a horse at
the races. Goodbye, Mr Tolman, Mr Sharp.

He leaves the office, happily singing a song.

TOLMAN (*Laughing*) Are you surprised, Mr Sharp?

SHARP (*Shaking his head and smiling*) No, Mr Tolman.
Not surprised at all!

'Are you surprised, Mr Sharp?'

INTRODUCTION

Once every ten weeks, office worker Towers Chandler dresses like a man with a million dollars, goes to one of the best restaurants in New York, and eats the most expensive food. One evening, he meets a girl . . .

CHARACTERS IN THE PLAY

Towers Chandler, an office worker
Marian, a pretty young girl
Sissie, Marian's sister
Marie, a servant
Jeff White, an office worker
Mrs Black, whose house Chandler and White live in
Waiter
Four other people in the restaurant

PERFORMANCE NOTES

Scene 1: The doorway of a house
Scene 2: A street corner in New York
Scene 3: A restaurant, with three tables and six chairs, two chairs at each table
Scene 4: Marian's bedroom, with a bed, and other bedroom furniture

You will need coffee, cups, plates, some food and some wine for the other people in the restaurant.

A Night Out

One dollar a week

The doorway of the house where Chandler has a room.
He is dressed in his best clothes, ready for his evening
out. He is going out as his friend, Jeff White, comes in.

WHITE   What are you doing this evening, Towers?

CHANDLER   (*Smiling*) Tonight I'm going to live like a man
with a million dollars!

WHITE   What are you talking about? You haven't got a
million dollars!

CHANDLER   How much money are you and I paid each
week, Jeff?

WHITE   Eighteen dollars. Why?

CHANDLER   And how much of that eighteen dollars do you
spend each week?

WHITE   All of it, of course.

CHANDLER   Well, I don't. Each week I save one dollar out
of my eighteen. Then, every ten weeks, I can buy
myself an evening to remember.

WHITE   What do you do?

CHANDLER   I put on my finest clothes, go to one of the best
restaurants in New York, eat the most expensive

food on the menu, drink the best wine, then take a taxi home!

WHITE (*Very surprised*) Why?

CHANDLER Why? Because it makes me feel wonderful to sit with some of the richest people in America, and to make them think that I'm rich, too.

WHITE You're crazy!

CHANDLER (*Laughing*) Perhaps I am!

Mrs Black comes in.

MRS BLACK Ah, Mr Chandler. I wanted to see you.

CHANDLER Good evening, Mrs Black. What a lovely evening.

MRS BLACK Lovely evening perhaps, but you haven't paid me for your room this month. When am I going to get the money?

CHANDLER Soon, Mrs Black. Very soon.

Mrs Black looks at Chandler's clothes.

MRS BLACK You can spend money on expensive clothes, but you can't pay for your room. Is that right?

CHANDLER (*Hurrying away*) Goodnight, Mrs Black!

SCENE 2
A pretty girl

A street in New York. Chandler is walking along the street when a girl, Marian, comes round the corner. She is wearing an old hat and a cheap-looking coat. She is moving quickly, walks into Chandler, and falls down.

MARIAN Oh!

CHANDLER Oh, dear!

Chandler helps her to get up. She has hurt her foot.

MARIAN My foot! I've hurt my foot.

CHANDLER Can you walk?

MARIAN I – I think I can.

She tries to walk, but her foot hurts too much.

MARIAN Oh! Perhaps—

CHANDLER I'll call a taxi to take you home.

MARIAN No, please. I'll be all right in a minute.

'Can you walk?'

Chandler looks at her carefully for the first time, and likes what he sees.

CHANDLER Your foot needs a longer rest, I think.

MARIAN Perhaps you're right.

CHANDLER I was on my way to eat by myself. Why don't you come with me? We'll have dinner together, and by then your foot will carry you home very nicely.

MARIAN But we don't know each other . . .

CHANDLER I'm Towers Chandler. Now that you know my name, come and have dinner. Then I'll say goodbye, or take you home if you prefer.

MARIAN But my clothes! They aren't—

CHANDLER I'm sure that you look prettier in them than anyone we shall see in the most expensive restaurant.

MARIAN Well . . . my foot does hurt. All right, Mr Chandler, I'll come. You can call me . . . Miss Marian.

SCENE 3
Chandler tells a story

Chandler and Marian are sitting at a restaurant table. A waiter is giving them coffee. There are two other tables near them. The people sitting at them are dressed expensively and are talking quietly while eating.

MARIAN That was a very good dinner. Thank you, Mr
Chandler. Tell me, what do you do?

CHANDLER (*Laughing*) Do? I ride my horses, go dancing,
travel to Europe. And then there's my boat.

MARIAN Haven't you got any work to do? Something
more – well, interesting?

CHANDLER My dear Miss Marian, there's no time for
work! Think of dressing every day for dinner, and
of calling at the houses of six or seven friends
every afternoon or evening.

MARIAN Yes – well—

CHANDLER Oh yes, we 'do-nothings' are the hardest
workers in the country!

MARIAN (*Sadly*) I see. Well, thank you for a nice time. I
must go home now. My foot is much better. I can
walk home. There's no need for you to come with
me.

CHANDLER Oh. Well, goodbye, Miss Marian.

*She gets up from the table and walks away. Chandler
watches her, sadly.*

CHANDLER (*Talking to himself*) What a wonderful girl! A
shop girl, perhaps? Why didn't I tell her the true
story of my life? Perhaps then . . . well, it's too
late now. Oh, how stupid I am!

SCENE 4

The right man for Marian

In Marian's bedroom. She is with her sister, Sissie. Both girls are sitting on the bed, talking excitedly.

SISSIE   It's two hours since you ran out in that old coat and hat. Mother has been very worried. She sent Louis in the car to find you. You *are* a bad girl!

Marie comes into the room.

SISSIE   Ah, there you are, Marie. Tell mother that Miss Marian is home again.

MARIE   Yes, miss. (*She leaves the room.*)

MARIAN   I only ran down to my dressmaker's to tell her to use blue on my new dress instead of red. Marie's old hat and coat were just what I needed.

SISSIE   You're crazy!

MARIAN   (*Laughing*) Everyone thought that I was a shop girl! It was wonderful!

SISSIE   Dinner is finished. You're very late.

MARIAN   I know. I fell and hurt my foot. I couldn't walk, so I went to a restaurant and sat there until I was better. (*She gets up from the bed and walks to the window. She looks down into the street below.*) We'll have to marry one day, Sissie.

SISSIE   Yes, that's true.

'I could love a man with kind blue eyes.'

MARIAN   We're rich, and mother and father will want us
         to marry somebody who is as rich as we are. But
         can I *love* a man like that?

SISSIE   Who could you love?

MARIAN   I could love a man with kind blue eyes, who
         doesn't try to make love to every girl he sees. But
         I could only love him if he has some important
         work to do in the world. Then it doesn't matter
         how poor he is.

SISSIE   You *are* crazy!

MARIAN   Perhaps. But, sister dear, we only meet men who
         ride their horses and go dancing. I couldn't love a
         man like that, even if his eyes are blue and he's
         kind to poor girls who meet him in the street.

INTRODUCTION

Who is the man who comes into Miss Martha's shop? Why does he buy two loaves of stale bread each time he comes? Miss Martha is very interested in him.

CHARACTERS IN THE PLAY

Miss Martha, a woman who sells bread and cakes in her shop
Blumberger, a man who comes into the shop for bread
Kelton, a man who works with Blumberger
Mrs Annie Green, Miss Martha's friend
Mrs Green's friend, a woman
A man in the shop
A woman in the shop

PERFORMANCE NOTES

Each of the four scenes happens in the shop. You will need four loaves of bread, some cakes, two packets of butter, a knife to cut bread, a painting, and some paper bags.

Two Loaves of Bread

The man who buys stale bread

Inside the baker's shop. Miss Martha is standing behind the counter, talking to her friend, Mrs Annie Green.

MISS MARTHA   He comes in two or three times a week, and he always buys two loaves of stale bread.

MRS GREEN   *Stale* bread?

MISS MARTHA   Always stale bread, never fresh bread. Of course, fresh bread is five cents a loaf, stale bread is five cents for *two* loaves.

MRS GREEN   And you think he's poor?

MISS MARTHA   Oh, yes, he is, Annie, I'm sure. One day I saw some red and brown paint on his fingers. 'He's a painter,' I said to myself.

MRS GREEN   Well, we all know that painters are very often poor. But can you be sure that he's a painter? Just because he has paint on his fingers . . .

Miss Martha takes a painting out from under the counter.

MISS MARTHA   I'm going to put this on my wall. If he's a painter, he'll see it and say something about it.

MRS GREEN   (*Laughing*) Very clever, Martha. But tell me, are you a little in love with this man?

MISS MARTHA   Annie! (*Laughing*) Well, perhaps a little.

SCENE 2

The painting on the wall

In the shop, the next day. The painting is now on the wall behind the counter. Miss Martha is putting some bread and some cakes into a man's bag. He gives her some money, then goes out of the shop. Mr Blumberger comes into the shop. His clothes are poor but tidy.

BLUMBERGER   Good morning. Two loaves of stale bread, please.

MISS MARTHA   (*Smiling*) Good morning.

She puts two loaves of bread into paper bags. While she is doing this, Blumberger is looking at the picture on the wall.

BLUMBERGER   That is a fine picture.

MISS MARTHA   Is it? I do love . . . paintings. Is this a good picture, do you think?

BLUMBERGER   The colour's good but the lines are not right. Good morning.

He takes the bread and leaves the shop. As he leaves, Mrs Green enters with a friend.

MRS GREEN   (*Excited*) Is that him?

MISS MARTHA   Yes!

MRS GREEN   (*To her friend*) That's the man! You know, I
was telling you about him. (*To Miss Martha*) Did
he see the painting?

MISS MARTHA   Yes! He knew at once that it was a good
painting. Oh, what kind eyes he's got!

FRIEND   And he only eats stale bread?

MISS MARTHA   Yes. He must be very poor. And he looks so
thin. Oh, I do want to help him.

MRS GREEN   (*Laughing*) You want to marry him!

FRIEND   Where does he
live?

MISS MARTHA   I don't know.
Some poor room
somewhere. But if
we marry . . .

MRS GREEN   He can come
and live here, with
you, over the shop!
Stop dreaming,
Martha!

FRIEND   What's wrong
with dreaming?
Sometimes dreams
come true.

MISS MARTHA   That's right!
They do!

'But if we marry . . .'

33

SCENE 3

Miss Martha tries to help

Two days later. A man and a woman are in the shop.
The woman is looking at the cakes, trying to decide
what to have. Miss Martha is putting some butter into a
bag for the man. She is now wearing her best clothes,
and her hair looks different.

WOMAN   Now, what shall I have?

MAN   (*To Miss Martha*) Thank you. Good morning.

He leaves the shop with the bag.

MISS MARTHA   (*To the woman*) Have you decided?

WOMAN   No, I—

She stops speaking as Blumberger comes into the shop.

MISS MARTHA   (*To Blumberger*) Good morning.

BLUMBERGER   Good morning. Two stale loaves, please.

MISS MARTHA   (*Smiling*) How are you today?

BLUMBERGER   I'm very well—

We hear an ambulance going past outside. Blumberger
and the woman both go to the shop door to look out.
Miss Martha quickly cuts into each of the stale loaves,
and puts some butter in them. She puts the loaves into
paper bags. Blumberger and the woman come back to
the counter. Blumberger pays Miss Martha. The woman
goes back to look at the cakes.

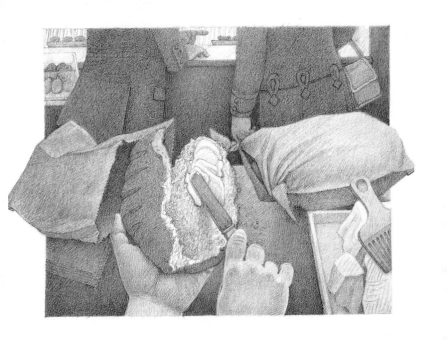

BLUMBERGER Thank you. Goodbye.

MISS MARTHA Goodbye.

WOMAN Now, what cakes shall I buy?

SCENE 4
A terrible mistake

Later that day. Miss Martha is in the shop with Mrs Green.

MRS GREEN So what did you do?

MISS MARTHA I put some butter in the bread! He didn't see
      me, of course. He was busy watching the
      ambulance. I had to be very quick.

MRS GREEN   How kind you are, Martha.

MISS MARTHA   I can't let him eat only stale bread, Annie.
He needs some good food, poor man.

MRS GREEN   What will he say when he sees the butter?
He'll know it was you who put it there.

MISS MARTHA   (*Smiling*) Yes, he will. (*She suddenly looks
worried.*) Do you think that he'll be angry?

MRS GREEN   No, of course not. Not if he's hungry. But I
must go. I'll see you tomorrow, Martha.

MISS MARTHA   Goodbye, Annie.

*Mrs Green leaves the shop. Martha begins moving one or
two things, making the shop tidy. Then she sits down
behind the counter and starts to read a book. Suddenly the
door opens, and Blumberger and Kelton come in.
Blumberger is angry, but Kelton is trying to hold him back.*

BLUMBERGER   (*Shouting at Martha*) You stupid woman!

KELTON   Wait! Blumberger!

BLUMBERGER   You stupid, stupid woman! Do you know
what you've done? You've ruined my work!

KELTON   Come on! You've said enough! It was an accident,
I'm sure.

*Kelton pulls Blumberger out of the shop. After a minute,
Kelton comes back again.*

MISS MARTHA   What's wrong with him?

KELTON   That's Blumberger. He's an architect. We work
together, in the same office.

'You've ruined my work!'

MISS MARTHA But what did I do wrong?

KELTON He's worked hard for three months now, on a plan for the new city hospital. It was a competition, and Blumberger was sure that he was going to win it.

MISS MARTHA But . . . why— ?

KELTON I'm telling you, miss. You see, he finished putting in the ink lines yesterday. When it's finished, he always rubs out the pencil lines with stale bread.

MISS MARTHA So that's why he wanted the stale bread!

KELTON Well, today – well, you know, that butter got right into the bread and when he tried to rub out the pencil lines – well, Blumberger's plan is ruined now, miss.

Kelton turns and leaves the shop. Miss Martha puts her head into her hands and starts to cry.

GLOSSARY

architect someone whose job is to plan new buildings

aunt your father's or mother's sister

bar a place where you can buy and drink alcohol

bet (in this play) to pay money, saying which horse will win a race. If your horse wins, you win; if it loses, you lose

butter soft yellow food that is made from milk

champagne an expensive French wine with bubbles in it

codicil something written after a will is already made, which gives more instructions about the money

competition a test in which people try to do better than each other

counter a kind of narrow table in a shop where you go to pay for something you buy

crazy mad, stupid

dream (in this play) to hope for something good in the future

fresh (of food) recently made and good to eat

ink coloured liquid used for writing, and sometimes for making pictures or plans

lawyer someone whose job is to help people with the law

line a long thin mark put on paper with a pen or pencil

loaf (plural **loaves**) a big piece of bread

necklace something pretty (and often expensive) that you wear round your neck

paint (*n*) coloured liquid used to make pictures

paint (*v*) to make a picture with paints

painting a picture

pretty beautiful, nice to look at

race (in this play) a competition to see which horse can run
the fastest

rub out to take off something that is written on paper

ruin to spoil or damage something so that it is no longer
any good

servant someone who works (for example, cooking or
cleaning) in another person's house

sir a polite way to speak to a man who is more important
than you

stale old and dry, not fresh

waiter somebody who brings your food or drink in a
restaurant

will a piece of paper that says who will have your money,
house and other things when you die

wine a strong drink made of grapes

One Thousand Dollars
and Other Plays

ACTIVITIES

Before Reading

1 **Read the back cover of the book, and the information on the first page. What do you know now about the people in these plays? Tick one box for each sentence.**

	YES	NO
1 Richard Rockwell's father is very poor.	☐	☐
2 Bobby Gillian's uncle is alive.	☐	☐
3 Bobby usually enjoys spending money.	☐	☐
4 Miss Martha wants someone to love.	☐	☐
5 Towers Chandler is very interested in money.	☐	☐

2 **Here are the four play titles. Which of the things, people or places below belongs to each play? Can you guess?**

All that Money can Buy   *A Night Out*
One Thousand Dollars   *Two Loaves of Bread*

a will	a necklace	Europe
a taxi driver	butter	a servant
a restaurant	a lawyer	a dancer
a painter	Broadway	a ring
blue eyes	an old hat	an architect

3 **What can you guess about these plays? Tick answers for these questions (you can tick more than one).**

1 What happens to Richard Rockwell in the play? He . . .
   a) learns to dance.
   b) loses his father's money.
   c) moves to another town.
   d) travels round Europe.
   e) marries the girl he loves.
   f) asks his father for help.

2 What happens to Richard's father in the play? He . . .
   a) loses all his money.
   b) helps Richard to marry.
   c) falls in love.
   d) dies.
   e) gives Richard a job.
   f) stops Richard's wedding.

3 What happens to Bobby Gillian in the play? He . . .
   a) drinks a lot of champagne.
   b) loses the woman he loves.
   c) gives $1000 to one person.
   d) asks a friend for help.
   e) finds a job.
   f) spends his money slowly.

4 What happens to Towers Chandler in the play? He . . .
   a) goes on holiday.
   b) meets a pretty girl.
   c) becomes rich and famous.
   d) breaks his leg.
   e) makes a stupid mistake.
   f) makes some new friends.

5 What happens to Miss Martha in the play? She . . .
   a) stops dreaming of love.
   b) ruins someone's work.
   c) starts a new business.
   d) feels sorry for someone.
   e) marries a kind man.
   f) loses all her friends.

While Reading

Read *All that Money can Buy*. Who said these words? Who were they talking to? And who or what were they talking about?

1 'Some young men pay more than a hundred dollars.'
2 'I love her, but how can I tell her?'
3 'All your money cannot make him happy.'
4 'I don't want to lose it.'
5 'Sorry, sir. But I can't.'
6 'That was a good day's work.'

Read *One Thousand Dollars*. Can you find and correct the mistakes in this passage?

Bobby's father, Septimus Gillian, wrote his will six months before he died. The will gave Bobby one thousand pounds to spend. At first Bobby wanted to buy a ring for his favourite singer, Lotta, but she asked for one which cost three thousand. So he decided to show the money to Miss Hayden, the sister of one of Septimus's friends. Bobby hated her, but she didn't love him, because she thought he only liked football, drank tea and rode horses. Bobby was unhappy when the doctors explained that she would get the rest of Septimus's money.

Read *A Night Out*. Choose the best question-words for these questions, and then answer them.

How / Where / Why

1 . . . much does Chandler save each week?
2 . . . often does Chandler go out to an expensive restaurant?
3 . . . can't Marian walk home?
4 . . . does Chandler take Marian?
5 . . . doesn't Chandler tell Marian the truth?
6 . . . is Marian when she is talking to Sissie?
7 . . . couldn't Marian love a man like Chandler?

Read *Two Loaves of Bread*. Match these halves of sentences and put them together using the words below.

because   but   so   which   while

1 Blumberger always bought stale bread,
2 Miss Martha saw some paint on his fingers,
3 . . . he only bought stale bread,
4 . . . he wasn't looking,
5 She hoped that he would be pleased,

6 she thought that he was very poor.
7 . . . she thought that he was a painter.
8 . . . in fact he was very angry with her.
9 she put some butter in his bread.
10 . . . was cheaper than fresh bread.

After Reading

1 **Anthony Rockwell has just finished talking to Richard (see page 3), and now he is talking to Kelly. Complete Kelly's part of the conversation. (Use as many words as you like.)**

ROCKWELL: Ah, Kelly. I've got a little job for you.

KELLY: Good afternoon, Mr Rockwell. What _____?

ROCKWELL: I want you to stop all the traffic on Broadway.

KELLY: But how _____?

ROCKWELL: Easy – just pay a lot of people to drive there!

KELLY: But what about _____?

ROCKWELL: You'll have to pay them too. Then they won't do anything to help.

KELLY: But it's going to _____!

ROCKWELL: Don't worry. I'll give you $5000 to start with.

KELLY: So when _____?

ROCKWELL: Tomorrow at 8.30 in the evening.

KELLY: Well, how much _____?

ROCKWELL: I'll give you a thousand for yourself.

KELLY: All right, _____.

ROCKWELL: That's wonderful, Kelly. Here's the money.

2 **Here is a different ending for *A Night Out* – a new Scene 4. Complete the passage, using one word in each gap.**

SCENE 4

Marian comes back into the _____ .

CHANDLER: (*Standing up*) Oh, Miss Marian!

MARIAN: I wanted to ask you _____ . Is it really _____ that you don't have a _____ ?

CHANDLER: No, I'm _____ , I don't _____ why I told you that.

MARIAN: Oh, good! I couldn't possibly _____ a man who has no _____ to do in the _____ .

CHANDLER: Does that mean, Miss Marian, that perhaps you could _____ me? But I must _____ you, I haven't got much _____ .

MARIAN: That doesn't _____ , because my _____ are very rich.

CHANDLER: I _____ you, Miss Marian! Will you _____ me?

MARIAN: Mr Chandler, my answer is _____ !

Which do you prefer, the ending in the book or the ending here? Explain why, or write a new ending yourself.

3 **Do you agree (A) or disagree (D) with these sentences from the plays? Explain why.**

1 'Money talks, right?'

2 'Sometimes dreams come true.'

3 'We all know that painters are very often poor.'

4 'A thousand dollars can be a lot or very little.'

5 'Money is nothing when you have true love.'

4 Perhaps this is what some of the characters in the plays are thinking. Which characters are they, and in which play? And what is happening in the play at this moment?

1 'He didn't see what I was doing! He's taken them! Oh, I *am* pleased! That'll fatten him up a bit.'

2 'But where can she be? She's been out for two hours! And she's wearing that old coat and hat! I hope she's all right.'

3 'Oh, he's so sweet! He buys me so many presents! I'd love a necklace like Della's. It'll look so much better on me than her!'

4 'I knew that ring would bring him luck. The dear boy! True love at last! I'm going to tell his father the good news at once.'

5 'So he thinks that giving money to the poor is a crazy idea? He only ever thinks of himself, that young man. Why did he ask me, anyway? Oh well, back to my book.'

5 Here are some new titles for the four plays. Which titles go with which plays? Which titles do you prefer, and why?

Money Talks	*The Rich Man and the Shop Girl*
An Architect's Plan	*Traffic on Broadway*
Dinner for Two	*The Quiet Woman*
Butter for Blumberger	*Lawyers Know Best*

6 Put these words from the plays into four groups, under these headings.

FOOD   NUMBERS   JOBS   FAMILY

aunt, bread, butter, cake, daughter, dressmaker, fifty, hundred, lawyer, million, painter, servant, sister, taxi driver, thousand, uncle

Now find all the sixteen words in this word search, and draw lines through them. The words go from left to right, and from top to bottom.

D	R	E	S	S	M	A	K	E	R	L	M	F
A	O	R	A	L	H	L	T	H	E	A	I	H
U	B	T	H	O	U	S	A	N	D	W	L	A
G	R	P	P	I	N	N	E	S	S	Y	L	F
H	E	S	H	E	D	U	N	C	L	E	I	I
T	A	X	I	D	R	I	V	E	R	R	O	F
E	D	B	R	I	E	S	E	R	V	A	N	T
R	N	G	S	T	D	C	A	K	E	U	O	Y
B	U	T	T	E	R	P	E	O	P	N	L	E
P	A	I	N	T	E	R	S	I	S	T	E	R

7 Look at the word search again and write down all the letters that don't have a line through them. Begin with the first line and go across each line to the end. You will have thirty-five letters, which will make a phrase of eight words.

   1 What are the words, who said them, and about whom?
   2 How does it make you feel about the speaker, and why?

ABOUT THE AUTHOR

William Sydney Porter (O. Henry) was born in North Carolina, USA, in 1862. When he was twenty, he went to Texas, where he worked in different offices and then in a bank. In 1887 he married a young woman called Athol Estes. He and Athol were very happy together, and at this time he began writing short stories. His most famous story is *The Gift of the Magi*, and many people think that Della in this story is based on his wife Athol.

In 1896 Porter ran away to Honduras because people said he stole money from the bank when he was working there in 1894. A year later he came back to Texas to see Athol, who was dying, and in 1898 he was sent to prison. During his time there he published many short stories, using the name 'O. Henry', and when he left prison in 1901, he was already a famous writer. He then lived in New York until his death in 1910.

Porter's stories are both sad and funny, and show a great understanding of the everyday lives of people, both rich and poor. He wrote about six hundred stories and made a lot of money, but he was a very unhappy man. When he died, he had only twenty-three cents in his pocket, and his last words were:

'Turn up the lights; I don't want to go home in the dark.'

OXFORD BOOKWORMS LIBRARY

Classics • Crime & Mystery • Factfiles • Fantasy & Horror
Human Interest • Playscripts • Thriller & Adventure
True Stories • World Stories

The OXFORD BOOKWORMS LIBRARY provides enjoyable reading in English, with a wide range of classic and modern fiction, non-fiction, and plays. It includes original and adapted texts in seven carefully graded language stages, which take learners from beginner to advanced level. An overview is given on the next pages.

All Stage 1 titles are available as audio recordings, as well as over eighty other titles from Starter to Stage 6. All Starters and many titles at Stages 1 to 4 are specially recommended for younger learners. Every Bookworm is illustrated, and Starters and Factfiles have full-colour illustrations.

The OXFORD BOOKWORMS LIBRARY also offers extensive support. Each book contains an introduction to the story, notes about the author, a glossary, and activities. Additional resources include tests and worksheets, and answers for these and for the activities in the books. There is advice on running a class library, using audio recordings, and the many ways of using Oxford Bookworms in reading programmes. Resource materials are available on the website <www.oup.com/bookworms>.

The *Oxford Bookworms Collection* is a series for advanced learners. It consists of volumes of short stories by well-known authors, both classic and modern. Texts are not abridged or adapted in any way, but carefully selected to be accessible to the advanced student.

———————————

You can find details and a full list of titles in the *Oxford Bookworms Library Catalogue* and *Oxford English Language Teaching Catalogues*, and on the website <www.oup.com/bookworms>.

THE OXFORD BOOKWORMS LIBRARY
GRADING AND SAMPLE EXTRACTS

STARTER • 250 HEADWORDS

present simple – present continuous – imperative –
can/cannot, must – going to (future) – simple gerunds …

Her phone is ringing – but where is it?

Sally gets out of bed and looks in her bag. No phone. She looks under the bed. No phone. Then she looks behind the door. There is her phone. Sally picks up her phone and answers it. *Sally's Phone*

STAGE 1 • 400 HEADWORDS

… past simple – coordination with *and*, *but*, *or* –
subordination with *before*, *after*, *when*, *because*, *so* …

I knew him in Persia. He was a famous builder and I worked with him there. For a time I was his friend, but not for long. When he came to Paris, I came after him – I wanted to watch him. He was a very clever, very dangerous man. *The Phantom of the Opera*

STAGE 2 • 700 HEADWORDS

… present perfect – *will* (future) – *(don't) have to, must not, could* –
comparison of adjectives – simple *if* clauses – past continuous –
tag questions – *ask/tell* + infinitive …

While I was writing these words in my diary, I decided what to do. I must try to escape. I shall try to get down the wall outside. The window is high above the ground, but I have to try. I shall take some of the gold with me – if I escape, perhaps it will be helpful later. *Dracula*

... should, may – present perfect continuous – *used to* – past perfect –
causative – relative clauses – indirect statements ...

Of course, it was most important that no one should see
Colin, Mary, or Dickon entering the secret garden. So Colin
gave orders to the gardeners that they must all keep away
from that part of the garden in future. *The Secret Garden*

STAGE 4 • 1400 HEADWORDS

*... past perfect continuous – passive (simple forms) –
would conditional clauses – indirect questions –
relatives with where/when – gerunds after prepositions/phrases ...*

I was glad. Now Hyde could not show his face to the world
again. If he did, every honest man in London would be proud
to report him to the police. *Dr Jekyll and Mr Hyde*

STAGE 5 • 1800 HEADWORDS

*... future continuous – future perfect –
passive (modals, continuous forms) –
would have conditional clauses – modals + perfect infinitive ...*

If he had spoken Estella's name, I would have hit him. I was so
angry with him, and so depressed about my future, that I could
not eat the breakfast. Instead I went straight to the old house.
Great Expectations

STAGE 6 • 2500 HEADWORDS

*... passive (infinitives, gerunds) – advanced modal meanings –
clauses of concession, condition*

When I stepped up to the piano, I was confident. It was as if I knew
that the prodigy side of me really did exist. And when I started
to play, I was so caught up in how lovely I looked that
I didn't worry how I would sound. *The Joy Luck Club*

The Importance of Being Earnest

OSCAR WILDE

Retold by Susan Kingsley

Algernon knows that his friend Jack does not always tell the truth. For example, in town his name is Ernest, while in the country he calls himself Jack. And who is the girl who gives him presents 'from little Cecily, with all her love'?

But when the beautiful Gwendolen Fairfax says that she can only love a man whose name is Ernest, Jack decides to change his name, and become Ernest forever. Then Cecily agrees to marry Algernon, but only if his name is Ernest, too, and things become a little difficult for the two young men.

This famous play by Oscar Wilde is one of the finest comedies in the English language.

Hamlet

WILLIAM SHAKESPEARE

Retold by Alistair McCallum

Why does Hamlet, the young Prince of Denmark, look so sad? Why does he often say strange things? His family and friends are worried about him. Perhaps he is mad!

But Hamlet thinks that he has discovered a terrible secret about a recent crime in his family. Now he has no time for Ophelia, the sweet girl who loves him, or his friends, who were at school with him. He sits alone, and thinks, and plans. What will he decide to do? Will he ever be happy again?

This famous play by William Shakespeare, written in about 1600, is one of the finest in the English language.

BOOKWORMS · PLAYSCRIPTS · STAGE 2

Romeo and Juliet

WILLIAM SHAKESPEARE

Retold by Alistair McCallum

What's in a name? Does it really matter if you are called Montague or Capulet? When Romeo, son of Lord and Lady Montague, falls in love with the most beautiful girl he's ever seen, he finds out that it does matter. It makes all the difference in the world, because both families hate each other bitterly.

For a time, Romeo and Juliet manage to keep their love secret. But when Romeo is sent away from Verona, and arrangements are made for Juliet to marry Paris, a friend of her father's, hope begins to die. Can any of their friends help the young lovers to be together for ever?

BOOKWORMS · PLAYSCRIPTS · STAGE 2

Much Ado About Nothing

WILLIAM SHAKESPEARE

Retold by Alistair McCallum

There are two love stories in this fast-moving comedy.

Brave young Claudio and Leonato's pretty daughter Hero are in love and want to marry, but Don John has a wicked plan to stop their wedding. Will he succeed, or will the truth come out? Will Claudio and Hero marry, after all?

Beatrice and Benedick are always arguing with each other, but how do they really feel? Perhaps they are more interested in each other than they seem to be! Their friends work hard to bring them closer together.

New Yorkers – Short Stories

O. HENRY

Retold by Diane Mowat

A housewife, a tramp, a lawyer, a waitress, an actress – ordinary people living ordinary lives in New York at the beginning of this century. The city has changed greatly since that time, but its people are much the same. Some are rich, some are poor, some are happy, some are sad, some have found love, some are looking for love.

O. Henry's famous short stories – sensitive, funny, sympathetic – give us vivid pictures of the everyday lives of these New Yorkers.

The Call of the Wild

JACK LONDON

Retold by Nick Bullard

When men find gold in the frozen north of Canada, they need dogs – big, strong dogs to pull the sledges on the long journeys to and from the gold mines.

Buck is stolen from his home in the south and sold as a sledge-dog. He has to learn a new way of life – how to work in harness, how to stay alive in the ice and the snow . . . and how to fight. Because when a dog falls down in a fight, he never gets up again.